Behind the Word
Bible Stories to Ignite Your Imagination
By Julie Anshasi

Giant Publishing Company
Lincoln, Nebraska, USA

2018 by Julie Anshasi

Published by Giant Publishing Company
Post Office Box 6455
Lincoln, NE 68506
www.giantpublishingcompany.com

Printed in the United States of America

Library of Congress Cataloging-in-Publication Data
Anshasi, Julie, 1963 -
Behind the Word – Bible Stories to Ignite Your Imagination
Fiction/Julie Anshasi
    1. Fiction-Christianity
    2. Bible

TXu 2-103-021

ISBN 978-0-9995873-3-1

Books by Julie Anshasi

Broken – Poems from the Holy Spirit –
Copyright 2017 - Winner of the 2021 Illumination
Book Awards Silver Medal

Some things are HOT! Some things are NOT! –
Copyright 2018

Why Did the Dinosaurs Die?
Copyright 2019

Winter in Eden
Copyright 2020 – Winner of the 2022 Illumination
Book Awards Bronze Medal

The Revelation of Jesus Christ
Copyright 2020

One Part Nonsense
Copyright 2020

Spiritual Exhaustion
Copyright 2021 - Winner of the 2022 Illumination
Book Awards Silver Medal

Forgiving Yourself
Copyright 2021

Behind the Word
Bible Stories to Ignite Your Imagination

Introduction

This book is a work of fiction. It is from my imagination, yet it is directed by the Holy Spirit. As a man of God who is very dear to my heart often says, the Bible is a summary. It is the word of God, but it does not and cannot contain every word of God. As the apostle John said, if everything that Jesus Christ did was written in a book, the world itself could not contain all the books. If every word of God was written in a book....

So, this is not the word of God. It is not adding anything to His word, nor is it taking anything away from it. It is fiction. It is about some of the characters mentioned or implied in the Bible, those who I describe as being "behind the word".

Some sharp-eyed readers may notice that the pronouns I use for Jesus Christ are sometimes capitalized ("Him" or "His") and sometimes are not capitalized ("him" or "his"). The reason for this is simple. Those characters in my book who believe He is the Son of God, refer to Him with capital letters, and those who don't, don't.

Praise the holy name of God. Praise the mighty name of Jesus Christ, the Son of the living God.

Julie Anshasi
Winner of multiple Illumination Book Awards
2018

For Abraham

May the Word always be inside of you.

Table of Contents

The nameless child...1
The pagan friend..3
The pig farmer...6
The donkey owner...11
The youngest Pharisee..14
The little child..18
The ship's captain..21
The priest...25
The bereaved wife..29
The marketplace shopper.......................................32
The servant..34
The innkeeper..38
The sacrifices..41
The nosy neighbor..46
The swine keepers..49
The carpenter...54
The bride...58
The granddaughter..63
The money changer...67
The idol...71
The lion...74
The widow...77
The fish...80
The seamstress...83
The soldier...86

The nameless child

I was born just a few days ago. In my very short life, I cannot remember a time when I was well. Fever wracks my tiny body. I twist on my bed in pain.

My mother comes into the room and gently lifts me. She presses me to her breast, but I am so weak and ill that I am not able to receive more than a few drops of nourishment from her breast. Tears are streaming down her cheeks and splashing on my tiny face.

My father enters the room where we are. My mother, still clutching me, falls to her knees automatically. "O king, live forever!" she chokes out through her tears.

My father's eyes are pools of exhaustion. He has not slept nor eaten for days. He places his hands gently on my mother's shoulders as she kneels on the marble palace floor.

"My lord, the king!" she sobs. "The child! I fear for the child's life! O king, call out to Jehovah for the life of the child!" She weeps uncontrollably.

"Dear one," my father says quietly. "I have cried out to my God day and night for the child, and I will continue. Who knows, perhaps the Lord will be gracious to us and spare the child's life?"

My father, king of Israel, quietly leaves the room. My

mother, still sobbing, rises from her knees and gently places me back on the bed. "O merciful God! Forgive me! Forgive me!" She runs from the room.

I can hear my father pacing in the adjoining room. He is saying, "Create in me a clean heart, O God, and renew a right spirit within me. Do not cast me away from Your presence! Do not take Your Holy Spirit from me! Restore to me the joy of Your salvation!" Then he, too, breaks off as sobs choke his words.

I would like to tell my parents that I forgive them. Even now, as I feel the last whispers of life ebbing from my body, I want to tell them that I love them and I hold nothing against them. I am too young to understand what they have done wrong, but it must be something very serious.

But it doesn't matter anymore...I am going now. Slowly I feel the pain leaving my body, being exchanged for light and peace. Yes, I am going. I am so far away now I barely hear my mother's screams as she runs back into the room. The servants are running in now, too.

But I am gone. I am not there anymore in that tiny, aching, feverish little body. I am at peace.

Behind the word: 2 Samuel 11, 2 Samuel 12: 1 – 23, Psalm 51

The pagan friend

I always liked Noah. He always had a cheerful word and a willing spirit. Noah was the kind of man who would help you with anything. He was the hardest working person I'd ever met.

I used to watch him, as he was hammering away at that enormous structure he was building. I'd asked him a lot of questions about it. He'd told me that judgment was coming on the earth, and everyone and everything would be destroyed. I must confess, that made me a little uneasy.

But only a little. Noah was always talking about God. I really wasn't much interested in his God. My wife and I, we have our own gods. We have a different god for every day of the week. His God just seemed too big to me. Our gods are manageable, at least. I'd stuffed one of them in my pocket as we ran out of the house.

My wife...oh, yes, my wife. We're separated by the water now. We had worked our way to the top of the highest hill we could find, which really wasn't that high when all was said and done. This hill has two plateaus on it. We were both so exhausted, you see. Water has been falling from the sky for days and days and days. I've never seen anything like it before. Who ever heard of water falling from the sky?

But Noah – he had said this would happen. Of course, I didn't believe him. As much as I liked Noah, I really just thought he was getting a little off in the head. That happens to some people when they get old.

Where was I? Oh, yes, exhausted. We had trudged through the mud, up the hill, up and up and up. Now, water has filled the little depression in between the two plateaus. So, she's over there, and I'm over here.

Bodies...so many bodies being swept along in the water. Hour by hour, there's more and more of them. It is a gruesome spectacle. Mercifully, most of them are face down, so I don't have to see the terror frozen on their faces as they drowned. Hundreds and hundreds of bodies - people, animals....and of course lots of debris. Because our houses have been broken up by the water. What had Noah called it? A flood, that's it. I didn't know what a flood was. No one did.

But somehow, Noah knew. Month after month, year after year, there he was, hammering away at that thing he called an ark. I didn't know what an ark was, either.

I guess it doesn't matter now. Because I haven't seen Noah for several days. He and his family went into that huge thing that he built, and then it just floated away on the water.

I look over at my wife. She is clinging to a spindly little tree, standing on her tiptoes. I hear her scream as the tree breaks and she, too, is swept away.

I am so exhausted. I haven't eaten or slept for days. All our crops are washed away; the fruit trees are underwater. And there's nowhere to lie down. It's just water. Water, water, everywhere.

A particularly swift gush of water temporarily lifts me off my feet. I panic and founder helplessly in the water. The little god I'd stuffed in my pocket has worked its way out, and is now floating away. Its wooden face is frozen in a permanent grimace.

I regain my footing. I should have taken all the gods with me! Maybe they could have saved us. But, we didn't think about that. As our house was filling with water, we just wanted to get to higher ground. Higher ground! How laughable that seems now. There's no ground high enough to escape this flood.

I look around. I seem to be the last one left. The water is up to my chin now.

I always liked Noah.

I wish I would have listened to him.

Behind the word: Genesis 6: 5 –22, Genesis 7

The pig farmer

Ah, these pigs! There are so many of them. Sometimes I am overwhelmed in looking after them. My wife is expecting another baby, I have my vegetable garden to tend to, and then, of course, these pigs. Why, just yesterday an old sow broke through the fence, and I was all day looking for her. I found her, rooting around in the trees. I drove her back, then I had to repair the fence. Ah, if it's not one thing, it's another.

But, I shouldn't complain. They are my livelihood, after all. And with this famine going on, I am lucky to have them. At least we can have roast pork with our vegetables. Ah, my wife's roast pork! There is nothing like it. My mouth waters just thinking about it.

What's this? In the distance I see a figure trudging toward me. His head is down, and his entire countenance seems dejected. I watch as he gets closer. Yes, I'm sure it's another person down on his luck. This famine has affected everyone. He shuffles up to me and stops. His head is down.

"Excuse me, sir," he says with downcast eyes. "I am in need of employment. Is there anything you can offer me? I will work hard...." his voice trails off.

I open my mouth to refuse, when a sudden thought strikes me. Here is the answer to my pig problem. I wouldn't have to pay him much, anyway. With this famine, people will work for next to nothing.

"Well," I say hesitantly. "I do need someone to look after my pigs."

"Pigs?" He steps back. His face betrays a horrified look.

Ah, yes. I should have known. A Jewish boy. I give him a good look, up and down. His clothing was, at one time, fine and costly. But now it is worn, and his shoes are almost completely worn out. He is dirty and unkempt. He looks as though he has recently come down quite a bit in the world.

"That is what I have to offer," I say flatly. "You may look after my pigs, or you may continue your journey. The choice is yours."

He looks at me, then down at the ground. His eyes dart from side to side. I can almost see his thoughts. Finally, he sighs.

"Yes, I will tend your pigs." He says it so quietly I have to strain to hear him.

"Very good," I say briskly. "Follow me."

I show the Jewish boy the pig pen. I show him the pile of bean pods from my garden, which is what the pigs eat. I warn him about the old sow who likes to break out of the fence. And then I go back to my house.

"Who was that young man I saw you speaking with?" my wife asks me, busy in the kitchen.

"Ah, just another person with a hard-luck story," I reply, off-handedly. Really, I am tired and I don't want to think about the lad any longer. I sit down and my children climb onto my lap. Ah, these little ones! What a blessing they are.

"I told him he could tend the pigs." I smile as I remember his face. "Pigs! Of all things! I think he's a Jew."

"Ah, well, this famine has certainly caused hardship everywhere." My wife shakes her head, wiping her hands on a towel. "I certainly hope you're not going to pay him much!"

"My wife," I say, amusedly. "As you well know, there is not "much" to pay him. He'll manage somehow, just as we all will."

That night I sleep peacefully, not concerning myself with the pigs and their wanderings, for once.

The next day I check on my young friend. He has dutifully pitched a new pile of bean pods into the feeding trough. I have not thought much about where he would sleep...ah, well. I have my own concerns.

Day after day, in between weeding and watering my garden, I watch the lad. He seems so downcast. Surely this could not be due just to his new employment! There must be something more to his misery.

After about a month, the boy approaches me as I work in the garden. I see him coming and straighten my bent back. He seems different, somehow. His steps are purposeful.

"Sir," he says, as he draws near. "I have reached a decision. I will no longer be able to look after your pigs. I have decided to return to my own country."

"And just where is that?" I ask warily. He tells me.

"But, lad!" I protest. "That is many days' journey from here! You will surely faint along the way – wait a moment! Just wait right here."

I rush into the house. My wife has just baked four loaves of bread. They are cooling on the table. I snatch one up and quickly wrap it in a cloth. Hurrying back outside, I thrust it into the boy's hands.

"Here, take this," I mumble. My conscience is bothering me a bit, truth be told. Perhaps I could have done more for the lad. Ah, this famine! Will it ever end?

"Thank, you, sir," he says, tucking the loaf under his arm. "I do appreciate your kindness. But I must be on my way."

He turns and begins walking down the path. I can hear him talking as he goes. It is almost as if he is an actor rehearsing his lines.

"I have sinned against you, and against heaven. I am no longer worthy to be called your son. Please make me one of your hired servants. Father, I have sinned." I hear him repeating the words until he is out of my earshot.

Ah, well, it's a funny world. I have my own concerns…

Behind the word: Luke 15: 11 - 32

The donkey owner

Things have been so exciting in Jerusalem lately! This Nazarene seems to have turned the city upside down. Everywhere he goes, crowds form.

I wish I could be in one of those crowds! But, I have my animals to tend to. These donkeys certainly have a mind of their own. If they don't want to go, they simply won't go, and no amount of prodding will get them to move.

I wonder...should I lead them out to pasture today? Then they would be away from the noise and bustle of all the crowds gathering for the feast day. But, I don't want to miss anything. If I stay here, I can feed them hay...I am in a dilemma as to which would be best.

I hear a noise behind me and turn around. A man with a kind face is untying one of my donkeys.

"And just what do you think you are doing?" I ask him indignantly.

"Pardon me," the man with the kind face says. "The Master has need of this animal."

Oh, the Master has need of him, is that it? I am going to tell this donkey thief just what I think of him. In fact, I am going to shout until the magistrate appears, and tell him just what is going on here. To steal another man's donkey! In broad daylight, no less! What is this world coming to?

"Yes, of, course," I hear myself saying, as though I am listening to someone else. "If the Master needs my donkey, of course you may take him."

What? Who said that? Surely not I? But, it was I who said it, and no one else. The kindly-faced man smiles at me. He finishes untying my donkey and begins to lead him away.

"Wait, wait!" I say, hurrying after him. "You must know, this donkey has never been broken to ride. No one has ever sat on him before. I fear that whoever tries may find himself tossed into the ditch in no short time."

The man smiles again. "I can assure you that will not happen. The Master said this was the donkey that He would ride into the city. He knows, above anyone else, what this animal will do."

He turns and continues leading my donkey away, who is plodding along as placidly as you please. He looks over his shoulder and says, "Thank you, sir, for your kindness to the Master."

I nod. I hardly know what to say. How did this come about? How could I have stood here like a fool and let this man take my donkey? How do I know if I will ever see it again?

But somehow, as I watch them walk away, that question loses

its significance. It doesn't matter anymore, because, well, simply because, the Master has need of him.

Behind the word: Mark 11: 1 – 10

The youngest Pharisee

I've been watching her. She doesn't know it, of course. But I have. I've suspected her for a long time. It is my duty to correct the people, to bring the people before the others and make sure they are brought back into line, whenever they transgress the law.

But this one – no, this one won't be brought back into line. She will be stoned. And, a good thing, too. She is an adulteress.

Yes, I've been watching her for weeks now. I've seen her go into that house where she has no business going. She can only be involved in evil. I feel it in my bones.

I am so thankful to be a Pharisee. God, I am sure, is glad to have me on His side.

Yes, there she goes, back into that house. I'll wait a few minutes, until the time is right. Today is the day!

That Nazarene – he has the people all stirred up. They think he is some kind of great prophet. Well, we will see what he has to say about this. I've heard him teaching in the temple, a time or two. He seems to know the law forwards and backwards, so surely he should know that adultery calls for stoning.

I see a few of my elder Pharisee friends passing by. "Psssst!"

I beckon them over. I whisper hurriedly into their ears. Their eyes widen in surprise. Yes, today is the day. Justice will be done. Not only that, but I will gain much favor and esteem in the eyes of the older Pharisees for noticing and rooting out this evil.

We collect in front of the door. On the count of three, we burst through. Yes, it is exactly as I thought. They are in the very act. Disgusting.

The man snatches up his robe and leaps through the window. I am hardly interested in him. It's the woman that I want. I grab her by her arm and pull her roughly to her feet. She is weeping and pleading with me.

"Quiet, you wicked woman!" I hiss at her. "You will certainly receive no mercy from me! You are a filthy sinner and all you will receive is stones!"

I yank her through the door and out into the sunlight. The older Pharisees follow us as I half push, half pull the naked woman through the streets. I hear gasps from people passing by. No matter. I am a Pharisee, after all. I am only doing my duty. Surely God is pleased with me.

We finally come to the temple. It is crowded with people, listening to that Nazarene. I push her through the crowd until she is standing directly in front of him. More gasps from the people.

I smile at the Nazarene while one of the older Pharisees explains what has happened. "Now, what do you say?" he asks him. I watch him closely. Maybe he will try to wiggle his way out of this one.

But he doesn't answer. He just stoops down and starts writing on the ground with his finger.

There are a few people in front of me; I can't quite see what is going on. But I hear another gasp – this time from the oldest Pharisee. His face is as white as a sheet, and he turns and quickly makes his way out of the temple, through the crowd. I push aside the people in front of me just in time to see the Pharisee's name written in the dirt...what's this? Next to a woman's name? What is the meaning of this? The Nazarene rubs it out with his hand.

Another Pharisee leaves, in a great hurry, and the Nazarene again rubs something out with his hand. I clear my throat. "Teacher, are you going to answer the question? What do you say should be done to this woman?"

He speaks very quietly now. "He that is without sin among you, let him first cast a stone at her."

Again, he is writing something in the dirt. The Pharisee in front of me utters an exclamation, and he, too, turns and rushes out of the temple. One by one, all the Pharisees leave.

The crowd is moving back from the Nazarene, but I press

forward. I see my name now, written in the dirt, with…no, this can't be. This can't be! I did that in secret! No one knew about that! I'd made quite sure of that. I'd paid that girl a handsome sum to leave town. There is no way this man could have known about it, no possible way. No one knew.

The woman we brought in is still standing there, naked, weeping.

An awful, horrible feeling of foreboding sweeps over me. In a moment, I see my life as a Pharisee, teaching the law, correcting the people, receiving admiring glances as I walk down the street – I see it all slipping away. If this man knows, who else knows?

Something needs to be done about this man. I turn and slowly walk out of the temple. This man, this so-called rabbi – he must be stopped. He must be stopped.

Deep within me, a searing hatred is kindled. I will not rest until this man is dead. Just as I did with that woman, I will watch him every day, until I see my opportunity. Then, I will strike.

I hate him. I hate him more than I've ever hated anyone.

Behind the word: John 8: 1 – 11

The little child

"No, no. We won't have any of that sort of thing, ever."

The Master is always so kind, but today His eyes are like a flame of fire. He had been teaching in front of the crowd, and my father had brought me forward. Of course, I am too young to understand all this. I just know that the Master's eyes are so kind, and I love Him so much.

But now, He seems almost fearsome. He has pulled some of His friends aside, and He seems to be scolding them very harshly. I cringe as I remember some scoldings my father has given me. I can tell His friends don't like it, either. Their heads are hanging down, and they look miserable.

He is saying, "You must allow the little children to come to me. You must not forbid them! This displays the kingdom of heaven, here on earth. I am telling you the truth! Whoever doesn't receive the kingdom of God as a little child receives it, shall not enter into it!"

I wonder, what is the kingdom of God? I've never seen God, and I think I know why. Sometimes at night I look up at the stars, and I think I understand that the Person who made all of them, must not be able to show Himself to me. My father read to me the story of Moses, how God had to hide him in a crack of the rock as He passed by. If He didn't, Moses would've just burned up, like the little pieces of kindling wood I gather for my mother. I do understand that. God is very big and powerful. He is so big and powerful, ordinary people can't see Him. I suppose a child like me could never see Him.

The Master is finished scolding his friends. He takes a little child standing near the front and lifts him up into His arms. He embraces him, then speaks a special blessing over him.

I understand about that, too. My grandfather spoke a blessing over me, right before he died.

The Master embraces another child and blesses him. Then, suddenly, He is right in front of me. I have to tip my head, way, way back to see Him, because I am not very tall. As He did with the others, He lifts me up and holds me gently in His arms. Now I am face to face with Him. I want to tell Him my name. I want to tell Him that my mother is making a rag doll for me, and it's almost finished. I want to tell Him so many things, but when I open my mouth, nothing comes out.

He has the kindest eyes I have ever seen. He is just a man, I suppose, but yet there is some kind of light that is all around Him and almost seems to be inside Him. I can't see the light with my little brown eyes – it's more like I feel the light. It's coming off of Him, and it's surrounding me.

And suddenly, I understand what the kingdom of heaven is. I understand that it is right in front of me. I understand that it is He – He is the kingdom of heaven.

And I have received Him.

I have seen God, after all.

Behind the word: Mark 10: 13 – 16

The ship's captain

How I love the sea! When I am on the land, I feel unsettled, as though I am somehow out of place. My ship is my true home. There, I am at peace. I look out at the endless sea, my ship rides the waves, and I find true happiness that I never find on land.

Every day is a new adventure. My ship carries goods all over the world. I sail to one coast and bring back spices. I sail to another and bring back rare cloth and unusual animals. I would have no other life than my life on the sea.

Today we sail from Joppa. We are heading to Tarshish. I call upon my gods, the stars, as I always do before we set sail. The stars guide me. They are always true. They have never failed me.

The last passenger boards. I overhear him talking with one of the sailors. I catch a few words – something about running away from God. I don't quite understand this. I could not run away from my gods – they are always there, shining above me.

We pull anchor. My men are very skilled and hard working. In no time, we are out to sea.

But out of nowhere, there is trouble. A sudden squall blows up. The sky, which had been clear and blue a moment ago, is suddenly dark and blustery. A stiff wind is blowing. My men are rowing, pulling hard, to no avail. My sturdy ship is tossed to and fro like a child's toy.

Fear grips me. I begin calling on my gods to save us. "Antares! Regulus! Show kindness unto us, O wise ones! Deliver us from this tempest!" My terrified men join with me, each one calling out to his god. In desperation they begin tossing our valuable cargo overboard.

I suddenly remember the last passenger who boarded. I had given no thought to him, until now. Where is he? I hurry below deck and find him, sleeping undisturbed. I shake him roughly.

"What do you mean, sleeping like this?" I ask him. "The ship is about to be broken in two by this storm! Call upon your god, man! Don't just lie there like a useless fellow!"

I take him by the arm and pull him above deck. The men have decided to cast lots. They are determined to find out which one of us has caused this catastrophe.

The lot falls on the sleeper. One by one the men turn and stare at him. He returns their stares. They begin peppering him with questions.

"What is your occupation? Where did you come from? Where is your family? Tell us, we beg of you, why this evil has come upon us?"

22

"I am a Hebrew," he says quietly. "I serve the God of heaven. He made the sea and the dry land."

The storm is raging all around us. The ship is heaving so much that we have to grip the sides to keep from losing our footing.

"Why have you done this – tried to run away from your god?" my first mate demanded. "What do you say should be done to you? This storm is surely because of you!"

The Hebrew man doesn't hesitate. "You must toss me overboard," he says firmly. "Then the sea will be calm. You are correct – this storm is my fault."

My men are debating among themselves. They clearly don't want to throw the man into the sea. They return to their oars and try valiantly to bring the ship to land. But it is no use. We have never seen a storm this fierce.

Prayers start going up. Yes, this has been the most unusual day of my life. I have never heard my men pray before. Oh, I have heard them chanting to their gods, but I have never heard anything like this.

"We beg of You, yes, we beg of You, O Lord, do not destroy us because of this man! Do not charge us with the crime of taking an innocent life! You, O Lord, have done as You pleased with him!"

A moment later, my men toss the Hebrew into the sea.

Instantly, the storm ceases. The wind stops. The waves that had been about to overcome my ship a moment before have flattened, and the sea is as smooth as silk. The clouds move away in a moment, and the sun shines brightly.

My men fall on their knees on the deck. One of them runs below and brings up a goat, which was to have been our supper. The goat is sacrificed to the Hebrew's God.

I remain on my knees. "God of this Hebrew man, You are the one true God. I will serve and worship only You, all the days of my life." My voice trembles as I make this vow. I forget all about Antares and Regulus. They did nothing to calm the storm.

I fear for the Hebrew man. I am certain he is already dead.

Who can run away from God? Where can he run?

Behind the word: Jonah 1

The priest

This is a dark, dark day in Jerusalem.

I have been a priest for many years. I'm an old man now. All of my life I have prayed and believed that I would see the Messiah in my lifetime.

I thought I had seen him. Jesus of Nazareth – He was the One. I was convinced of it.

Until today. Today, they nailed Him to a cross. He is hanging there now.

Crowds gathered to watch His mock trial and execution – they always gather when anyone is crucified. Not I. I watched in horror as they beat Him. I watched Him carrying that heavy cross, to a place outside the city – the place of the skull. Then I couldn't watch anymore.

I ran back to the temple. I went into the holy place and burned some incense. I called upon Yahweh as the tears rolled down my face.

How could this be possible? I saw Lazarus, alive and well, walking and talking, a week after I had spoken over his body as he was buried! I saw the blind beggar at the gate – blind since birth, and now he sees. I saw so many miracles the Nazarene had done. How could it be over now? How could it end like this? I had thought He was the Messiah.

Suddenly it is dark, very dark. The lamp I have lit barely penetrates the thick blackness that has settled over everything. I rush outside. One of the other priests has just come from the hill.

"What is happening?" I ask him. He shakes his head.

"The sun no longer shines," he says, his voice trembling. "It's because of the Nazarene."

"What does this mean?" I ask. Now my voice is trembling, too. It is so dark I can barely see my hand in front of my face.

"It is the judgment of God," he says. His face looks like that of a hunted animal. "We must repent. All of Israel must repent!" He turns and quickly makes his way through the outer court.

I go back into the temple, back into the holy place. "Yahweh!" I cry out. The agony I feel is almost unbearable. "Yahweh! Have mercy on Your people! Forgive us, O Lord!"

I hear a very loud noise. It is so loud and so sudden, I gasp in fear. It is the sound of cloth ripping. I whirl around and face the holy of holies.

The veil has been torn in two, from the top to the bottom.

My knees knock together. The room begins to whirl around me. I clutch the edge of a table, because I am about to faint.

The veil separating the holy place from the holy of holies, is sixty feet high. It is about four inches thick. And it is now torn completely in two, its jagged halves trailing the floor.

No human hand could have torn the veil. I am the only one in here, anyway. From the top to the bottom...from God to man. The holy place is now wide open. The place where a priest is allowed to go only once a year, is now open to anyone. Open to anyone…

Something is forming in my mind, something that perhaps I had always known, or should have known, something that my years in the priesthood had taught me. God's desire has always been to dwell in His people. God has never wanted a separation from His people, but our sins have always separated us from Him.

Until today. Today, there is no more separation. Today, it is finished.

I have been a priest for many, many years. My account of these happenings is true. I will spend the rest of my life telling my fellow priests, the Pharisees, the scribes, and the people, what happened in the temple today.

We, priests and people alike, now have free access to God.

The veil in the temple is torn in two.

Behind the word: Luke 23: 44 – 45

The bereaved wife

Today started like any other day. But it is nighttime now, and I am crying. I am crying so much the sobs convulse my body.

My husband left early this morning. He was a servant of king Nebuchadnezzar. Whatever the king asked, my husband did, without question.

We used to joke, privately and quietly, that maybe the king was becoming a little too grandiose. He seemed to have the highest possible opinion of himself. When he had this gigantic statue built, that seemed to prove it. Ninety feet high? Made of gold? And all of us must bow to it, when we hear the music playing.

Now, I understand that he is the king. Kings are not like the rest of us. But still, he is a man, after all. My husband and I used to smile privately about this. Of course, we wouldn't dare speak about it openly. We value our own necks too much.

But, I learned today, there are some people who don't value their own necks. Those three Hebrew boys. What odd names they have! They refused to bow before the statue.

I wonder if they knew what trouble they would cause by their stubbornness. I wonder if they even thought about it. Why, oh why, couldn't they just have bowed down, as all the rest of us did?

But, they didn't, and the king was infuriated. He told his servants to build up the fire seven times hotter than usual. Of course, the servants obeyed.

Just as my husband obeyed. He always obeyed the king. The king commanded him to seize one of those Hebrews by the ankles, and my husband obeyed. Another servant seized the boy by the shoulders. Others laid hold of the other two boys, and they ascended to the top of the furnace, to throw them in.

But the fire was too hot. It was much too hot. It was so hot, no one could bear the heat of it. No one could get close to it.

King, did you know you were sending my husband to his death? Did you consider that, when you gave the command to heat the fire seven times hotter? Or did it not matter to you at all? Did you believe you must have your revenge, at all costs?

My husband, my dear one. My soul's delight. The heat was too much for you.

The heat from that fire killed all the men who threw the Hebrews in. All of them.

Yes, now it is nighttime. When I awoke this morning, the sun was shining, and I was happy. I embraced my husband as he was leaving for the day. Now, it is dark, and I am crying, and crying, and crying.

I am a widow.

Behind the word: Daniel 3

The marketplace shopper

What a lovely day it is today in Azotus! My relatives are coming to visit my family today. There is so much to do!

I wanted to get to the marketplace early, to buy a chicken. I must rush home, pluck it, dress it, and roast it before my family arrives. I must also make sure the children are bathed and have clean clothes to wear, my house must be tidied up – oh, there are a dozen things to do before my relatives arrive.

I stop at a vendor who is selling figs. My uncle does love figs…hmmm, should I buy some? The price the seller is asking seems a bit high.

I grasp one of the figs and hold it up to the light. Sometimes these tricky vendors try to sell produce that has mold on it. That would never do! I would be shamed in front of my uncle…no, that would never do. I hold the fig up and scrutinize it carefully.

Suddenly, I no longer see the fig I am holding. Instead, I see a man standing where no man was standing a moment before. He is dripping wet from head to toe, and his arms are raised above his head. His eyes are closed.

"Oh, glory to God! Praise the holy Name of the Most High God, and praise the mighty Name of Jesus Christ, the Son of the living God!" he is saying.

I drop the fig. The fig seller behind me doesn't even notice that. He gasps, staring at the man, and his face is white. Other shoppers across the lane have stopped dead in their tracks, their mouths open and their eyes widened.

I rub my eyes. What is this? Is this a ghost? People don't just appear out of nowhere! And why is he dripping wet?

The man lowers his hands and opens his eyes. He starts a bit, then looks around. He sees the crowd of morning shoppers all staring at him. He looks down, all around, then up. Then he smiles again. He turns to me.

"Pardon me," he asks pleasantly. "What is the name of this city?"

"Azotus," I say faintly.

"Azotus. Azotus. Well, well. Your ways, O God, are not my ways." He smiles again, gathers some folds of his robe in front of him, and squeezes them. A little torrent of water rushes out onto the street.

He nods his head, turns, and walks away with a purposeful stride. We all watch him go, leaving wet footprints behind him.

What a tale I will have to tell my relatives when they arrive!

Behind the word: Acts 8: 26 – 40

The servant

"We are leaving tomorrow at daybreak," my master says quietly. "Load the camels with food and provisions for at least fourteen days."

That is all he says. He quickly turns to go, as though he can't bear to speak another word.

"Master, wait." I hurry after him. "May I ask the purpose of this journey?"

He turns slowly. I notice that his eyes are red-rimmed.

"The lad and I go to worship," he says quietly. Then he leaves.

So, the other servants and I load the camels. I feel, somehow, that I should not ask any more questions. Going to worship God is certainly not a new thing for my master. I have never seen him like this, however.

We leave at daybreak – I, the master, his son, and another servant. I have always counted myself blessed to serve this man. He loves God and serves Him with all his heart. Because of his faithfulness to God, I and my entire family have been blessed, along with all of his other servants. As he is faithful to God, I am faithful to my master. I respect and admire him.

The camels plod on and on. The sun gets hotter and hotter. We stop for water, whenever we find a spring, and I refill the containers. We will certainly need this water.

The master says very little. His son, a handsome, strapping young lad, seems to sense his father's mood and also says very little. We seem to be a somber group on this journey.

Finally, we see the mountain in the distance. The master turns to me and the other servant.

"Remain here," he says quietly. "The lad and I will go to the mountain and worship. We will start our journey home when I return."

I watch them walking slowly toward the mountain. The strong young lad is carrying the wood, and his father is carrying the fire. Of course, they must be planning a sacrifice. Odd that they brought no sacrificial animal…

An uneasy feeling begins to envelop me. I try to shake it off. I can't really place it, anyway. It is simply a feeling that something isn't right. "When I return…" that's what he'd said. Not "we."

The other servant and I build a fire as evening approaches. We pass a few hours by singing some songs from the old days – songs to cheer a weary soul. But somehow, we don't seem very cheerful.

Days pass. Another night approaches, and we prepare to sleep. A small sound, a clattering pebble being dislodged, causes us to look up. The master and his son are returning, making their way toward our camp. As they get closer, I stare at their faces.

The master is a study in contradictions. Awe, sorrow, joy, reverence, stupefaction – all seem to appear on his face at the same time. The lad is no better. He stares off at the horizon and doesn't reply when spoken to.

After a long pause, the master finally says, "We will camp here tonight. We will start our journey home at daybreak."

He and the lad move off some distance from the rest of us. They appear to be in earnest conversation.

I so want to know what they are discussing! I catch only a word here and there, floated to me on the still night air. "Obedience...sacrifice...love...forgive." They talk and talk for such a long while.

Then the master takes his son into his arms in a full embrace. They stand there like that for some time, arms wrapped around each other, and I hear the sound of faint sobbing on the night air. Then, they part, and start walking back to camp. I quickly turn around so they don't think I am spying on them.

We are all tired. It was a long journey to reach this place, a long time waiting while my master and his son walked to the mountain, and another long, uneasy time while we waited for them to return. We have to begin another long journey tomorrow. We stretch out on our mats. The lad's mat is next to mine.

We lie there, side by side, staring up at the stars. Finally, he speaks.

"My father loves God," he says, simply. "He truly, truly, loves God."

"Yes, indeed he does," I reply warmly. "Your father is very faithful."

"No, you don't understand," the lad replies, impatiently. "I'm telling you that my father loves God more than he loves anyone or anything else. My father will go to any length to obey God's commands. Any length!" He falls silent again. Finally, he says, "I have more admiration for my father now than at any other time. I pray, someday, that God may give me the grace to be like him."

"He will," I reply firmly. "I know it."

Behind the word: Genesis 22: 1 – 19

The innkeeper

I see them coming at a distance. Business has been slow today, and I have been idly looking out the window. As they draw nearer, I see a man walking, leading a donkey with another man sprawled across it like a sack of overripe vegetables. The man leading the donkey stops in front of my door.

"Can you please look after this man?" he asks me. "He has been beaten by thieves, and he is in a bad way. He needs someone to tend his wounds, give him a clean bed, and feed him some broth. I am on a journey to a far country, and he is in no condition to travel with me."

"I don't know," I speak hesitantly. "I certainly don't want to get mixed up in any trouble." I peer more closely at the wounded man. He certainly is in a bad way! His face is swollen and bruised; his eyes are mere slits. He appears to have a broken nose, and probably several broken ribs as well.

"The thieves are long gone," the first man says firmly. "Cowards," I hear him mutter as he begins pulling the wounded man off the donkey. I rush forward to help him, and we carry him into a vacant room and lay him on the bed as gently as we can. Nevertheless, he winces in pain.

"It is getting late," the first man says. "I will stay here tonight as well and tend him during the night."

For the first time, I take a very close look his face. Then I look at the face of the man on the bed. This makes no sense.

"Sir, you are a Samaritan," I say in disbelief. "And this man is clearly a Jew. Why are you helping him?'

"Because no one else would help him," he says flatly.

That seems to be enough. I drag another mat into the room, then hurry to the kitchen to prepare some food for my guests. I wish my wife were here! But, she has gone to visit her relatives. I prepare a simple stew for the first man, and broth for the wounded man.   Together, we take turns putting spoonsful of broth into his mouth. He doesn't speak, but his eyes convey his gratitude.

The next day, the first man rises at dawn. I am used to rising early, and am already in the kitchen when he comes in. He digs into a pouch at his waist. "Here, use this money to take care of his food and lodging." He gestures toward the room where the wounded man is sleeping. "I will be headed back this way in a few days, and if you need more, I will give it to you then. I must be on my way." He moves out of the darkened room, back into the misty light of early morning.

"Yes, I will look after him," I say, still hardly believing what has transpired here.

"Thank you," he says simply. "And I will pay you whatever you require when I come back."

Perhaps he repeated this to me, to reiterate his sincerity. I don't know. I watch him ride off and shake my head. I wonder if my wife will believe me when she returns? The Jews have no dealings with the Samaritans!

What a strange world it is!

Behind the word: Luke 10: 30 – 37

The sacrifices

I remember the garden very well. It was indescribably beautiful. We were all friends in the garden, and we all talked freely with one another, every day. I talked to Leopard, who was my special friend, every day. We all loved one another deeply.

Leopard was the Man's special companion, and I was the Woman's. But there was no jealousy or envying of someone else's place. We each had our own place, and we each fit in our place beautifully.

The Woman and I would go for long rides. She would climb up on my strong back, and we would gallop for miles. We never got tired. The sun was always warm on our faces, and the grass sang beneath my hooves as I sped along. Yes, the grass sang. The plants, animals, insects, trees, moon and stars, all had their own songs. And we all sang together, and we all understood one another. Yes, it was a beautiful place.

After a long ride, we would come back. We would slow down to a leisurely pace, and the Woman would reach up and pluck a piece of fruit off of one of the trees. All the trees bore fruit in the garden, and when one fruit was picked, another one grew in its place instantly. She would offer me the fruit, and I would eat it with anticipation and joy. All the fruit in the garden was delicious, and each one had its own flavor. Some were sweet. Some were salty. Some had a creamy flavor. All were delicious.

We would spot the Man, wrestling with Leopard, and they would both be laughing. It was a game they used to play. Leopard would hide in the tree branches, and the Man would whistle nonchalantly and amble along beneath him. "Leopard, where are you?" he would call. Of course, the Man knew where Leopard was. It was just a game. Leopard would chuckle softly, then drop noiselessly down onto the Man's back. They would roll over and over in the soft grass, until the Man started tickling Leopard behind the ears, and they would both burst into laughter.

After watching them for awhile, and laughing ourselves, the Woman would slide down off of my back and go to the Man, and they would embrace. They were made for each other, you see. Then Leopard and I would nuzzle one another, and lie down with the other creatures under the stars.

I remember the day the Man named us all. The Lord gave him that responsibility. We all came to him, respectfully, and he named us, one after the other. I waited in great anticipation to see what my name would be. When the Man said, "You shall be called Zebra," my heart leaped with joy. I knew that was the perfect name for me. I wanted no other name, and I was honored to carry the name the Man gave me.

Every day was unique. Every day there was something new to see, and something new to do. I knew the Lord had created each one of us, but I could not remember a time when I had not been. I could not remember a time when the garden had not been. Life, to me, was the beautiful garden, my many, many friends, the Man and the Woman, and the Voice of the Lord, Who spoke to all of us, every day.

But that was before. That was before The Day.

The Lord, in His great mercy, took away the pain of that day. The memories are still there, but He took the pain. That's what He does.

Leopard and I knew something was different that day. We didn't know the word "wrong" then, but if we had, we would have known that something was wrong. A cold wind blew through the garden. We heard the Voice of the Lord speaking to the Man. His Voice was different than it had been before, and we didn't understand why.

Then the Lord came to us. His Voice was filled with deep, deep sorrow. We didn't know what sorrow was, either, but He explained it all to us later. He told us that He needed our skins.

"Of course, Lord," we both replied instantly. "Whatever You need, please, You are welcome to it."

We didn't understand what we were saying. We didn't understand any of it, until later.

It was mercifully quick. The Lord cut Leopard's throat and mine by speaking a word. So much blood! I had never seen blood before. Leopard and I lay motionless in that vast pool of blood.

Instantly, He took us far away. We were in another place. He allowed us to look down on our former selves. I had often seen my reflection in the clear pools of the garden, and I knew that I was very beautiful. But now...I was just a bloody, lifeless form. My beautiful black and white stripes were gone. Leopard's beautiful spots were gone. So that is what the Lord meant when He said He needed our skins.

From the place where we were, far, far away, I heard the Man and the Woman screaming. I had never heard screaming before. It was a horrible sound. Leopard and I looked down and saw the Man, now wearing Leopard's coat, and the Woman, now wearing mine, kneeling next to our bodies. They were screaming and crying. The Woman was tearing at her hair.

Nothing like this had ever happened in the garden before. In a moment, the beautiful life we had known was gone. But the Lord is so merciful. He made another place for Leopard and me. This place is not the garden, but it is beautiful, like the garden. It is a place very far away from the garden. He gave us both new skins.

Even as we look, we see things starting to change. Some of the leaves are falling off of the trees. Some of the animals are starting to bite one another. The Lord, in His mercy to us, closed the window into that place, so we could no longer see it.

Just before the window closed, I saw the Man and the Woman leaving the garden. They were still sobbing. The Woman looks so strange, wearing my skin. It doesn't fit her. The Man looks so odd, wearing Leopard's skin.

And they are both so sad.

Behind the word: Genesis 2:9, 19, 3:9 - 24

The nosy neighbor

"What are those boys doing?" I fret. I have been watching them through the window all morning. It just doesn't make sense.

"And what are *you* doing, wife?" my husband demands. "Surely you have much better things to do than to stare out of the window all day!"

"Those boys – you know, the widow's sons – the one who lives down the street. Well, they've been going from house to house gathering jars and pots all morning. I don't understand it!" I exclaim.

"And why is it your business?" my husband asks.

"Doesn't it seem odd to you?" I reply. "What can they be doing with all those vessels?"

Just then there is a knock at the door. I rush to open it. Maybe it is one of our neighbors. Maybe she will have an explanation for this odd behavior of the widow's sons.

No. It is the widow's eldest son! "Pardon me, ma'am," he says politely. "My mother has sent me to request a favor of you. May we please borrow any jars or pots that you are not using? We will return them later, of course."

"How much later?" I want to know. "I will need them for the harvest, you know. And may I ask what your mother wants with them?" I artfully slip in that last question as I am gathering up my spare pots.

"We will certainly return them in time for the harvest," he replies politely. "As for why she wants them…" his voice trails off.

Now my husband has become interested. He leans forward in his chair and fixes the lad with an interrogatory gaze.

"It is the prophet," the boy says, finally. "He told my mother to borrow as many vessels as she could, from all of our neighbors. He didn't explain why."

My husband is a godly man. He fears the Lord. "Wife," he says, rising from his chair, "you have not gathered enough vessels. Surely we have more than this!"

"There are some out back, near the spring" I say grudgingly. "You may help yourself to them, as you like. But just how much do you know about this prophet?"

Before I can speak another word, my husband places his hand over my mouth. I notice his hand is trembling. "Please, take all that we have, and go quickly. The prophet is waiting."

The boy gathers up the vessels and leaves. I watch him go, peering out of the window. "I'm going to get to the bottom of this," I mutter. My husband is sitting in his chair again, shaking his head.

I wait until the boy is out of sight, then I tiptoe out of the house, looking this way and that. Good, no one is watching. I hike up my robe and race down the street. No doubt my husband would say I look undignified! I come to the widow's house. Again, looking furtively in all directions, I creep up to the window and crouch beneath it. Cautiously, I lift my head and peer through a crack in the shutters.

The widow's house is filled with jars, pots, vessels, and urns of all types. And she is pouring oil into each one of them. But, the container she is pouring from is very small. She never refills that small container, she just keeps pouring, pouring, pouring oil into every available pot.

The oil never runs out.

I watch for a long, long time. When I finally leave, she is still pouring.

What does this mean? I have never seen anything like this in my life.

Behind the word: 2 Kings 4:1 - 7

The swine keepers

"Wake up, lazybones!" I nudge my companion in the ribs.

"Ahhh… mmphh," is all I hear from my friend.

"No, you must wake up!" I am insistent. "There is quite a ruckus brewing over by the pigs."

My fellow herdsman finally opens his eyes. He had been taking advantage of a warm afternoon by having a nap under a tree. "Uhhh…what is it?" he mumbles. "I had been having the most wonderful dream!"

"Never mind your dream," I say unfeelingly. I scramble to my feet and peer over at the next hill. Yes, it's that madman again. My friend and I have learned the hard way to give him a wide berth. This man is insane – stark, raving mad. Sometimes we hear him screaming in the middle of the night, and it makes the hair stand up on the back of my neck.

It looks like some people have come to try to take him, again. When will they ever learn? I once saw him break the chains that he had been bound with. Chains! Only madness brings with it such unnatural strength.

But, wait…they are not binding him. I see One of them placing His hand on the madman's shoulder. He is actually allowing Him to touch him? What is the meaning of this?

An uneasy feeling grips me. "We'd better go see to the pigs," I say abruptly. "We don't want any trouble."

My friend and I hurry over to where the little crowd is gathered around the insane man. He is speaking in a hollow, echoing voice. It sounds like many voices at once, but he is the only one speaking.

"We know You!" the voice, or voices, speak. "What do we have to do with You? Please leave us alone! Don't send us into the abyss!"

The pigs seem uninterested in the drama unfolding. They are busy rooting around in the earth, as pigs do, looking for roots and worms, grunting and snuffling.

"Send us into the pigs!" the man screams.

The pigs? Wait, I am the one in charge of these animals! Whatever this insane man is proposing, which I don't understand at all, should have nothing to do with these pigs. I step forward to lodge my protest.

But it is too late.

Without warning, the pigs start squealing and screaming. Some of them rear up on their hind legs and paw the air. They start shaking their heads, violently from side to side, as if to rid themselves of insects. One pig turns and viciously attacks the pig next to him. And suddenly, as if they are not a herd of two thousand, but acting as one, they began to race blindly toward the cliff.

"No!" I shout. "We have to stop them!" My fellow herdsman races after me as I pursue the pigs. They are running at breakneck speed. I would have said, before today, that it would be impossible for pigs to run so fast.

They reach the cliff long before we can catch up to them. In a massive, writhing tide, they go over the edge.

I stop, panting. My friend, out of breath, reaches my side, and we both stand there, staring over the edge of the cliff. The pigs are drowning in the sea. In a moment, the last one disappears from view beneath the waves.

We slowly turn and face each other. My friend looks as if he has seen a ghost. I'm sure my face looks no better. "How – how are we going to explain this?" he stammers falteringly.
"I don't know," I say. And really, what explanation can we give?

We are silent as we make our way back to the village. I have the unhappy task of telling the swine owner that his entire herd has been lost, and the reason why. It is such a fantastic tale! So fantastic, that instead of beating us, he accompanies us back to the hill to see for himself. Several of his relatives and neighbors come with us.

When we get there, the insane mad has been washed, and is wearing a clean robe. He is sitting quietly on the grass, along with a few other people. They are listening to the Man who had touched the insane man earlier.

I pull one of the men aside. "This is the owner of the swine," I say, indicating my master. "I have explained to him what happened, but he would like to hear what you have to say."

I step back a few paces. The man tells my master what happened to his pigs. Thankfully, he says the same things I had said earlier.

My master steps aside and has a hurried conversation with the people who came with him. They are a fidgety crowd! I hear a few words, and they are not complimentary.

My master comes forward and clears his throat. He speaks loudly, so everyone will hear him. "You must leave this place," he says to the Man and His friends. "It is best for all of us if you go - and go quickly."

The Man Who is speaking stops. He reaches down and offers His hand to the insane man and helps him get up. But he is not insane anymore! He looks like an entirely different person! I can scarcely believe this is the man who used to cut himself with stones and screech like a demon at all hours of the night. He looks perfectly normal, now. He doesn't even look like the same man.

"Yes, we will go," the Teacher says quietly. He turns and walks in the opposite direction of the village. The man who is now sane follows Him, begging Him to allow him to go with them. They converse for awhile, then the healed man turns and begins walking back to the village.

My master watches all of this. He shakes his head. "Just how am I supposed to replace two thousand swine?" he demands of me. I lower my head in disgrace.

"That man is nothing but trouble," he says. "Good riddance. I hope he goes far away and never comes back."

I turn and watch the Man and His friends walking away. Trouble? I don't think so.

Behind the word: Mark 5:1 - 20

The carpenter

The sun beats down mercilessly on my back as I hammer, pound, saw, and hammer some more. We have been working at this structure all day, and it is now almost seventy-five feet tall.

As a carpenter, it has been my pleasure to build many fine things. I have built tables, chairs, bed frames, and cabinets. I have always taken pride in my work. But this job has been distasteful from the beginning. I have never built gallows before.

"Why does he want this, anyway?" my fellow worker grumbles. He stops to take a swig of water from the wineskin at his side.

"Shhh!" I look uneasily around me. "It is not our place to question him. He is second in command to the king. No doubt some vile criminal is about to be hanged."

"Or, more likely, some poor fool who didn't bow low enough to suit him as he passed by," my friend mutters.

"Quiet! You'll get us in trouble! I cannot afford to lose this position. I have a family to feed, you know." I wish my friend would just shut his mouth and get on with the job.

"Ah, you worry too much." He tosses his hammer down to the ground. And indeed, as I look up, down, and all around this massive structure, I see that we are finally finished.

We climb slowly down to the ground and look up at the monstrosity we have built. It makes me shudder. I hate to think of someone hanging up there, his body impaled, birds swooping down and plucking at his eyes…

No matter. I have done what the king's highest officer has asked me to do.

But doing one's duty sometimes comes with a price. That night, I cannot sleep. When I do sleep, I am tormented by dark dreams. Darkness, screams, bodies swaying on gallows…I awaken briefly, then sleep again, only to be engulfed with more dreams. I finally awaken for good as the dawn creeps through the window.

"Oh, what a wretched night!" I exclaim.

"Yes, I heard you groaning in your sleep," my wife remarks. "You must have had some unwelcome dreams."

"I certainly did," I reply. "It's that gallows I had to build yesterday. I pray I will never have to build another one as long as I live!"

It's a new day, and it is very busy. A rich customer had asked for two matching bedframes, with two matching cabinets. The work on the gallows had put me behind on his request, so now that that distasteful task is finished, I throw myself into my work with vigor. I want to put the memory of the gallows far, far, behind me.

I work and work all day with hardly a pause. My wife brings me something to eat, and I eat while standing up and hammering. If I do well on this job, the rich man may recommend my work to his friends.

I do not realize how late it is until I find myself straining to see the wood and my tools. Darkness is falling. Suddenly, I hear footsteps running outside my door, then more footsteps. A crowd is forming near the gallows.

I fling open the door to my workshop. "What is happening?" I demand of a lad running by.

"The king's chief man is being hanged!" the boy shouts over his shoulder as he runs.

"The...king's...chief...man?" I say faintly.

When he had ordered us to build the gallows, surely...surely, it was intended for someone else...?

"Lad, wait!" I catch the boy by his garment. "What happened? Why is he being hanged? What did he do?"

"He was plotting against the queen and her people!" The boy is bouncing up and down in his excitement. "And I hear that he even tried to force himself on her!" He dashes off.

It isn't until later that I learn the whole truth. And when I do, it makes me tremble. If it had not been for the Hand of God, an innocent man would have been hanged on the gallows that I helped to build. But God intervened.

Those who plot evil against others will have that same evil returned on their own heads. Those who dig a pit for others will fall into it themselves. And those who lay a snare for others, will be trapped in that very snare.

I have seen this firsthand.

Behind the word: Esther 5:14, 7:5-10

The bride

I have waited for this day for so long! I awaken with great anticipation. There is so much to do!

The house is full of relatives, of course. My little cousins are racing around, squealing and trying to catch one another. My grandmother has been cooking and baking for days on end to feed all of the family who have traveled such great distances. Everywhere is confusion, excitement, busyness, laughter, scolding, tears of joy, and many wise words from my grandfather.

Today is my wedding day.

"Can someone please get these children out of here?" I ask in exasperation. "I am trying to get ready, and they are underfoot."

My sister appears out of nowhere and gently shepherds the children out of the room. I am combing my hair with shaking fingers. I am so nervous! Everything must be perfect today.

I ponder all of the things which must be done today. My husband's uncle is in charge of the wine, my best friend will be arriving shortly with the perfume, my mother has chosen the jewels that I am going to wear...oh, how I hope I have not forgotten anything!

My groom is so handsome. When he asked my father for my

hand, I could scarcely believe it. All the girls in my village had admired him. But of all of them, he chose me. When my father told me, I almost fainted.

That was a year ago. We waited a year, according to our tradition, for the actual wedding to take place. I wonder if he is as nervous as I am?

***

After the ceremony, my husband and I spend our first night together. My nervousness vanishes as he holds me in his arms. We both thank God for bringing us together.

The morning dawns bright and clear. Now the feasting begins! My husband's family has prepared a massive feast. As we enter the banquet room, a great cheer goes up. Everyone is so happy! There is not a face here without a smile on it. There is something about weddings – something that makes them more special than any other celebration.

There are so many people here! Some of them I don't even know. My mother has invited every uncle, every cousin, every distant relative of a relative in our entire family.

My husband's uncle approaches us, smiling. He pours my groom and me a glass of wine. I taste it. It is delicious – the best.

We feast, laugh, talk, and feast some more. This is the

happiest day of my life. Until...

I spy Uncle having a tense conversation with my mother. He appears to be apologizing, and my mother looks as though she is near tears. My husband gets up and goes over to where they are talking. He comes, back, shaking his head.

"What is wrong, dear one?" I ask him. He sighs and shakes his head again.

"It seems that we have run out of wine," he tells me.

"Run out of wine?" I exclaim. "How can this be possible? What does your uncle have to say about it? This is our wedding! I wanted everything to be perfect!" Now I find myself also near tears.

"I think he underestimated how many people would be here," my husband says sadly.

I blink to hold back my tears. My guests must not see me crying at my own wedding feast. There must be some solution to this.

There He is, sitting across the room. I lift my head and see my older brother, seated with a group of men. I don't recall inviting those men; no doubt my mother invited them. My gaze is drawn to my brother; indeed, I can't seem to look away.

When we were young, my brother always seemed to know what to do. He didn't play with us that often; when our chores were finished, He would often go away by Himself somewhere. He always seemed to be listening for something, or Someone. In the inevitable childhood squabbles that occurred in my large family, He always had the solution.

Our mother is talking to Him now. They are in deep conversation. I see Him shake His head. He turns to the men that are with Him, and gestures toward some water pots.

Watching Him, I almost forget about my dilemma.

I see the men pouring water into the pots. My brother beckons my husband's uncle to come over.

Uncle puts the dipper into one of the pots and draws out some liquid. I watch him taste it. A wondering expression comes over his face.

"This is the finest wine I have ever tasted," he exclaims.

Wine? The containers were filled with water, not wine. I saw that with my own eyes.

Uncle draws more liquid out of the water pots and goes around, refilling everyone's glasses. He comes to my husband and me and refills our glasses. He is humming a tune and smiling from ear to ear.

We taste the wine. It is even better than the first taste of wine we had at the beginning of the feast. It indeed, is the best wine I have ever tasted.

How can this be? What did my brother do?

I nudge my husband. "Did you see what happened to the water in the water pots?" I have lowered my voice to a whisper.

"Yes, I saw it," he answers slowly.

"How do you explain it?" I ask my new husband. He turns and looks at me full on.

"I can't," he says. We gaze at each other in bewilderment.

I had always wanted my wedding to be unique, unlike any other girl's wedding.

And it was.

Behind the word: John 2:1 - 11

The granddaughter

I am sad. None of my sisters want to play today. And I can't ask any of my friends, because our parents probably won't let us play, anyway.

They always keep us inside when there's a crucifixion.

I don't understand crucifixion. I ask my father to explain, but he won't. All he says is, "Those evil Romans! Those evil Romans!" Then he starts, and looks over his shoulder, this way and that, in case one of the evil Romans might be lurking nearby.

The Roman soldiers – they scare me. Whenever I see one, I run and hide behind a tree, or rock, or sometimes my older brother. They are mean. They have mean faces.

I heard the adults whispering earlier. They always whisper when they don't want the children to hear. But I caught a word here and there. They were talking about the Master.

Oh, how I love the Master! All the children love Him. We flock to Him. We are drawn to Him, like little bees to honey. He is so kind to all of us. Sometimes the other adults shoo us aside or tell us to stop laughing so loudly – adults are always doing things like that. Not the Master. He always stops and talks to us. He hugs us and lets us sit on His lap. I love Him so much.

The adults are whispering again. Let them whisper. I am sad that I had no one to play with today, and I am tired, and I am going to bed.

***

"Papa, may I please play outside today?" I am impatient. Surely the crucifixion is over now. I don't know how long a crucifixion lasts.

My papa's eyes are red. He sighs. He looks this way and that. Slowly, he nods. "Yes, little one. You may play outside today. It has been three days…" His voice trails off.

I race across the road to my friend's house. She must have been watching for me out of the window, because her door flies open and she races out to meet me. "Oh, I am so happy to see you!" she exclaims. "I have been so lonely and sad. Did you hear about the Master?"

"What about Him?" I am excited. Maybe He is planning to pass by our homes today!

My friend's eyes are also red. "He was crucified three days ago by the Roman soldiers. He is dead." Her head droops and a tear rolls down her cheek.

Dead? The Master? No, it can't be! What did He do wrong to make them kill Him? So, this is why the adults were whispering.

"No! No!" I scream. Tears are rolling down my face now, too. I forget all about playing with my friend. I turn and stumble blindly back in the direction of my house.

How could they kill the Master? Those evil Romans! Those evil Romans!

At home I curl up into as small of a ball as I can, and I cry. I cry for the Master. I cry for myself and my friends, who will no longer get to see Him and play with Him. I cry and cry.

"Hush, child," a gentle voice is saying. I lift my tear-stained face and look into the eyes of my grandmother. I am so distraught that I do not stop to think how strange this is.

"Oh, grandmother," I sob. I fling my arms around her neck. "They have killed the Master. He's dead! I'll never see Him again!" I am almost hysterical in my grief.

"Child," she says, lovingly but firmly. "He is not dead. I saw Him with my own eyes less than an hour ago. He came to us, where we were, and spoke to all of us. He told us so many things! Child, don't you see? He is the Messiah! He is the One our people have been waiting for, for so many years! He is the One!"

The Messiah? My parents always talk about the Messiah. They say He will come and liberate my people from oppression. They say He will set us free. They say He will show us the way to Jehovah.

I sit back on my heels and wipe my face with the back of my hand. My grandmother smiles at me so tenderly. She gets up and kisses the top of my head, just as she always used to do…

"Grandmother, where are you going?" I still am not quite myself. I still don't quite see how...

She laughs softly. "You know, child," she muses. "I am not exactly sure. He asked us to come with Him, and most of us did. But He didn't tell us where we were to go after that. But one thing I know for certain."

Grandmother stands in the doorway of our little house and smiles at me a final time. "One thing I know for certain!" she repeats. "I mean to find out! And wherever He tells me to go, that's where I will go!" She blows a kiss at me, and quietly leaves the house. I hear her humming a little tune as she walks.

I sit on the floor for quite awhile. I think about the Master. I think about the Messiah. Mostly, I think about my grandmother.

My grandmother…who I loved so much…

Who died two years ago.

Behind the word: Ephesians 4:8 – 10, 1 Peter 3:18 – 19, Matthew 27:51 - 53

The money changer

"How dare you!"

I am so angry I am beside myself. I start screaming and cursing at this fellow – this so-called rabbi.

"How dare you!" I scream at him again. "Who do you think you are? Who gave you the authority to come in here and disrupt everything like this?"

He doesn't answer me. Indeed, I don't think he hears me. He goes from table to table, overturning each one. Coins fly in all directions. Some of the pigeons have escaped and have fluttered away.

My fellow merchants hardly know what to do. Some of them are terrified and simply run away. Others are scrambling to pick up their coins, retrieve their straying animals, set their tables back up.

Now he has pulled out a whip. One by one, he starts whipping the merchants in the temple courtyard. Now he has simply gone too far.

I am so enraged I don't know what I am doing. I rush at him. His back is to me, and his whip is moving from side to side. He seems to sense that I am behind him, that I am almost upon him. He turns with a quick movement and lashes his whip in my direction.

He handles the whip expertly. I am facing him, but the whip snakes around behind me and strikes my back. It is extremely painful. I stop in my tracks as the pain sears through me. I step back a pace or two.

As the other merchants see their fellows receiving lashes, they retreat quickly. But he seems to have an uncanny knowledge of where everyone is. One is cowering beneath his table – zing! The whip finds him. As others are turning to flee, they are lashed across their backs as well.

I have never seen such chaos in the courtyard. This man must be stopped.

I try again. This time I approach him slowly. He too, turns slowly toward me.

"Look here," I say in what I hope is a reasonable tone. "You can't treat us like this. We are simply…"

"It is written," he says quietly. "My father's house is a house of prayer. But you have made it a den of thieves." His eyes bore into mine.

I stare at him defiantly, then I look away. I cannot bear to look into those eyes. They seem to see right through me.

All of my anger has dissolved away. I have nothing more to say to this man. "We are simply performing a valuable service," was what I had meant to say earlier. Now, this trite statement seems wholly inadequate. There is nothing I can say to him that is true. Somehow, he has cut through all my reasonable arguments with one word.

Den of thieves? I have to admit he is right. I do overcharge people. I do it frequently. It had never bothered me before. Now...

I shuffle back to my table. I set it upright. I gather my scattered coins and place them in my sack. I stand there, in the courtyard, next to my table.

He is finished now. Everyone has been driven out. He turns and looks at me again. I wish he wouldn't.

We stand in the temple courtyard, facing one other. I am now terrified of this man. A few minutes ago I was ready to kill him.

I must do something. I can't stand here forever. I approach him cautiously, sack in hand. "Here," I say abruptly. "Please put this in the temple treasury." I press the sack into his hand.

He says nothing. He takes the sack from me, and slowly turns to view the temple. I hear him speaking quietly, so quietly, under his breath.

"I have always done Your will, my Father. I have cleansed Your temple. I have made things right again."

I cannot move fast enough to get away from this man. He unsettles me. He makes me feel so uneasy. Exposed! Yes, that's how I feel. Exposed, as though I had been stripped naked, right there in the courtyard.

I rush back to my table and pick it up. I rush out of the courtyard.

I don't know what I am going to do tomorrow.

Behind the word: John 2:13 - 17

The idol

They gloat as they bring it in. They set it up carefully in front of me, and then leave. "We have taken the Hebrews' ark!" I hear them say. They are almost beside themselves with glee.

I study this new item dispassionately. I do everything dispassionately. I am an inanimate object.

This new thing they've brought in – it's different, somehow. It glimmers with a beautiful golden hue. It seems to radiate light, but, of course, that is impossible, because it, too, is an inanimate object. But it is different somehow…

Long ago, they made this special place for me and set me in it. They come, often, and bow down before me, chanting. If I could smile at them I would. But I can't. I was carved from a block of stone, and my mouth cannot form a smile.

I'm not exactly sure when it happened, but after some period of time, It came and started living inside of me. That's something that most people don't understand about idols. Those Things, those Beings that live in the darkness, often come and inhabit us. They crave worship and adoration, and since we are the uncaring recipients of these things, They come in. That way, They can have it all.

It doesn't matter to me. I have no feelings.

That night, the power strikes. It is so overwhelming that I cannot remain upright. I fall to my face in front of the ark. Its golden sheen glimmers off of my back. Of course, it was not really I that fell. It was the Thing that had taken up residence in me. It couldn't stand before the presence of the ark, so we both went over.

No matter. I don't care.

There is quite a disturbance when they find me on my face the next day. They lift me up, reverently, and dust me off. They carefully set me back in my original position, saying some extra chants as they do so.

But it is all to no avail. That night, I fall again. This time the power from the ark is so strong that my head and my hands are chopped off. My hands fly in opposite directions. My head falls off and rolls over and over, coming to rest in the corner. My broken and decapitated body falls, once again, before this much greater power.

If I had the capability to wonder, I would wonder at this. What is the power contained in this ark? Why does it cause idols to fall?

When they find me in the morning, they are very upset. There is much shouting and commotion. They pick up the ark and carry it out in haste. Some of them are limping. They all seem to be suffering and in great pain and distress. It seems the power emanating from the ark has afflicted them, too.

The Thing that was in me also left in haste. I suppose it had to find another home. That should not be too difficult. There are thousands of us, scattered all over the world. Some are stone, some are wood, some are metal. All are lifeless objects that men have created to worship.

If I had the capability to laugh, I would laugh at this. How can a man worship something that he has formed with his own hands? How can he expect anything from it? And yet, he does. He calls it his god.

No matter. I have no interest in these things, one way or another.

I am an inanimate object.

Behind the word: 1 Samuel 5

The lion

I am so ravenously hungry that I am almost beside myself. They have not fed me or my companions for a week. I resent them.

I also resent being in this place. I am the king of the jungle. I am supposed to roam free and hunt my own prey, not have it delivered to me by those fools. I pace back and forth, back and forth. I am angry, agitated, and extremely hungry.

Night is falling. I roar more loudly than I have ever roared before. My fellow lions begin roaring with me. The sound is heard for quite some distance beyond our den.

Suddenly, there is activity above us. Yes, it's true! They are throwing us some fresh meat! I race over to where it falls in an awkward heap.

Something is different, somehow. Something is wrong. This fresh meat smells bad to me. I approach it cautiously. It springs up and moves away from me, its back to the wall. I continue approaching. I sniff it. The other lions join me. We circle around our dinner, sniffing it.

I have never smelled such a horrible stench! But I have to make sure. I am so hungry! I lick it. It leaves a horrible taste in my mouth.

Some of the other lions also try licking this new prey. I see the disgust on their faces as they back away.

I don't understand this! We have had this type of prey many times. Usually it is delicious! This one...this one is just nauseating.

The overwhelming hunger I had felt just minutes ago vanishes in a moment. The other lions and I retreat to a corner of the den, lie down together, and promptly fall asleep.

The next day dawns, and we awaken. It is very early. I hear one of them calling from outside, in that strange language that they all use, that I don't understand. Our prey, or what was to have been our prey, answers. I hear the stone being rolled away, and they toss a rope down to it. It grabs the rope and they quickly remove it from our den.

Well, good riddance. That thing smelled bad and tasted bad.

Just as quickly as the hunger had left me last night, it returns. I roar in frustration and anger.

As if in answer to my roar, new prey is tossed in. There are so many of them this time, not just one. And oh, how wonderful they smell! What an enticing aroma!

My companions and I snatch this bounty from the air, before it ever hits the ground. We make short work of it. For the next few minutes the air is filled with the sound of breaking bones and tearing flesh.

That's my favorite sound.

When we are finished, there is not much left. A nub of bone here, a spot of blood there. Ah, that was a wonderful meal.

We are all satisfied now. We return to our favorite corner, lie down, and go to sleep.

Behind the word: Daniel 6:16 - 24

The widow

Things have been hard since my husband died. But I don't feel sorry for myself. There are others who are much worse off than I.

My husband left me a little money. I have spent it as wisely as I could, making it stretch as far as it will go.

My children have been a help to me, as much as they are able. Of course, they have their own families to feed, and money is scarce on all sides. But what we lack in money, we make up for in love and respect. I am grateful that God gave them to me.

I wish my husband had lived long enough to see the Messiah. I have seen Him. He teaches in the temple, almost every day. I go to listen to Him often. When I am downcast, when I am encumbered with worries, His words calm my soul. Just being in His presence makes every care flee away.

I want to go listen to Him today, but I don't want to go empty-handed. I go into my kitchen and retrieve my money pot, which I keep hidden behind all my other pots. I take it down from the shelf.

Just a few pennies…that's all that's left. I smile a sad smile. Yes, I certainly did stretch the money as far as it would go. No one could accuse me of being extravagant!

For a moment I am overcome with grief once again, remembering my husband and the years we spent together. How I loved him. And now, all that is left is these few pennies.

I dry my tears and wash my face. I am going to the temple. I am going to hear the Master teach. I must not appear before Him with a tear-stained face. Somehow, everything will work out. Jehovah has always taken care of me, and He always will.

I make my way to the temple. It is very crowded, as usual. It seems sometimes that the entire city turns out to hear Him teach.

I find a spot near the back and try to be inconspicuous. I am not the best-dressed person here, not the best educated, and certainly not the wealthiest! I am just an ordinary widow woman, who loves to hear the Master teach.

He is talking about the scribes today. I wonder how they feel about that! He is certainly not being complimentary.

"They love to wear long robes, and love it when the people greet them in public. They love to have the best seats in the synagogues and at feasts. But they extort money from widows – the very people who can least afford it! And they make a show of praying loudly, for a long time, to give the impression that they are the most pious of all people. They shall receive great damnation."

Oh, my. He is certainly right about the scribes. That is exactly how they behave. I have seen the sneering looks on their faces when I give my small offerings. I see some of them glaring at Him right now.

Offerings…yes, it is time to give our offerings now. I look down at the pennies in my hand and breathe a whispered prayer.

"O God, You know and You see what is in my hand. Please, take this offering and do with it as You see fit."

I wait until the others have finished. There are many rich people here today, it seems. After they have all finished putting their money in the treasury, I make my way to the front, and cast in my coins.

Yes, that is all I have left. No more money in my hand, no more money in my money pot at home. But God will provide.

As I turn to go, I see the Master smiling at me. He beckons to the men around Him, and gestures in my direction. Under most circumstances, I would feel embarrassed by this, but today, I feel joy. I feel light, as though by casting my few coins into the treasury, I had cast off all my burdens.

He knows me, and He understands.

Behind the word: Mark 12:38 – 44

The fish

Oh, what is that delightful glittering thing in the sand? I must have it.

I swim up to it and snatch it up in my mouth. It is quite heavy. I actually feel as though I am now swimming slower, because the weight of it is dragging me down. Nevertheless, I swim on.

In a way, it is a bit disappointing. I had expected it to taste delicious, but it doesn't. It doesn't even seem to be any kind of food at all.

Yes, we find all kinds of things in the sea that aren't food. Those creatures that live up there, on the dry land, always seem to be losing their belongings in here. I am so glad that I am a fish, and I have no belongings.

I join a school of my fellows and we swim along companionably. They are all opportunistic feeders; whenever a smaller fish or insect comes in their path, they immediately snatch it up in their jaws. Normally I would do that, too, but today I have the glittering thing in my mouth, and I know if I open my mouth to snatch at anything else, I will lose it.

Now, that seems odd to me. Why do I care, anyway? It doesn't taste good. It is slowing me down. And yet, I feel that I must keep it for some reason. Certainly, no other fish in this sea has ever discovered anything as glittering as I have discovered today. I feel a bit proud of my find. I swim alongside another fish and nudge him with my fin. I open my mouth just a crack, to show him what I have. His eyes widen.

"Where did you get that?" he asks.

"Over there," I mumble, gesturing with my fin. I am careful not to open my mouth too wide.

"That is certainly something!" he says. "That is very special."

Now I am really proud. I smile at him as he swims away.

What's this? The surface of the water above me is broken by another glittering object. Oh, what is it? I must have it. I open my mouth carefully, and quickly close it around this new glittering delight.

This one is not as delightful as the one I found earlier. I find myself flailing on the end of a string, being drawn out of my beautiful liquid home, up into the suffocating atmosphere of the creatures that live above. My mouth is forced open, and both objects are removed quickly. Just like that, I am tossed back into the sea.

I feel quite dazed. I swim slowly for some time, not even knowing where I am going.

"What happened?" My friend swims by me again.

"I'm not sure," I say, slowly. "I was out of the water for a short time – it was horrible! I couldn't breathe. Then suddenly, I was back here again."

"Oh, my father warned me about that," my friend nods his head wisely. "You have to watch out for those shiny things. You never know when you might be taken captive! It's a dangerous world we live in." He looks to his left and right fearfully, then quickly swims away.

Yes, it is a dangerous world. I am a bit sad that I lost my beautiful treasure that I had found, but only a bit. Somehow, I feel that I have fulfilled my destiny. I have done something that no other fish has ever done.

Oh, what's that? I must have it!

Behind the word: Matthew 17:24 - 27

The seamstress

"Do you understand? I want you to make it exactly as I have specified."

"Oh, yes, master." I have no doubt that I can do as my master has asked. I am an expert seamstress, and I feel very confident that this new garment will turn out exceptionally beautiful.

My master nods, gives me a quick smile, and exits the room. Well, I have no time to waste. I must begin immediately.

I begin sorting through all my scraps of linen. Yes, I have many different colors, that is good. Now, I cannot just randomly piece them together; there must be a distinctive and beautiful pattern. I sit back and contemplate the pieces. I move one here and another there. I survey the result, shake my head, and begin again. This must be perfect.

After a long time, I have the pieces arranged in a pleasing pattern. I step back and look at them from across the room. Yes, that looks beautiful. Many, many different colors, all arranged in a graduated pattern, from light to dark, and with the various color families grouped together and complementing one another – oh, yes, this will be beautiful. I take up my needle and thread and begin sewing.

There is something about this garment that I cannot put my finger on. It is different from the other garments that I have made. It almost seems holy, somehow. I shake my head. Oh, now I am just being fanciful. It is simply a coat that my master has asked me to make for his son.

I do worry a bit, though, about how his other sons will react to this. Even though I am just a servant, it is impossible not to see how much the master loves this son. This one has always been special to him. But, that is not my concern. I must attend to the task at hand.

Day after day, I sew and sew. It is a good thing that sewing is my chosen profession! I have always loved it, and I have always enjoyed giving the finished garments to their owners. There is something about creating a beautiful coat out of simple scraps of linen…it seems like a divine calling to me.

I am finally done. I respectfully approach the master, coat in hand, and show it to him. He beams with joy when he sees it.

"Well done!" he exclaims. "That is exactly what I wanted! It is even better than I had imagined it would be."

I smile modestly and say nothing. I watch him hold the coat up and look at it from all angles.

"Yes, this is exactly what I wanted. Well done!" he repeats, and hurriedly leaves the room.

I wish to see the son's reaction to this gift. I follow the master at a discreet distance, then quickly hide behind a tent flap.

"Father, it is beautiful!" the boy is saying. "How can I thank you? I never dreamed I would wear a coat like this, ever in my lifetime."

The father is smiling, his son is smiling, everyone is happy. Everyone, that is, except the master's other sons. In the days to come I hear their unkind remarks on several occasions. I suppose that's how it is in many families…

I am happy that this garment is finished. I can now go on to other tasks.

It is wonderful to have made a coat of many colors. I am sure it is the only one in the world.

Behind the word: Genesis 37: 3-4

The soldier

I never dreamed this would happen. In all my time in the military, through all my years of training, I had prepared for every possibility. I was ready for anything. I could face anyone, at any time. I was not afraid.

Now…I am leaving town, under cover of darkness, ashamed and humiliated.

They had told us to go to the garden, in the darkness, so of course we went. A soldier doesn't question; he just does what he is told. We found Him there, alone, praying. Those men that were always with Him were some distance off, sleeping.

He asked us who we had come for, so we told Him. He said that He was the one we were looking for. As soon as He spoke, I fell over on my back. I don't know why. All He had said was, "I am He." Just three words, and I couldn't stand upright.

We all went over, all six hundred of us. Six hundred soldiers, lying on our backs, flattened by three words.

Why was it necessary to send so many of us? He is just one man, after all. His friends all ended up running off, anyway. They seem a useless bunch to me.

Somehow, we recovered ourselves, stood up, and arrested

Him. We led Him out of the garden.

I wasn't a part of what happened next. I was thankful for that. It doesn't take six hundred men to strip one man, scourge Him, and pound spikes into His hands and feet. I was assigned elsewhere, so I hurriedly left.

But there's no getting away from Him. Two days later, I am told to guard His tomb. Some warning about grave robbers.

We relieve the guards that had been there before us. They leave hurriedly, looking over their shoulders. We come in the third watch and stand guard outside the tomb for hours. That is nothing. A soldier does as he is told.

It is still dark when the women come on the third day. They are carrying something; something having to do with their burial customs. I don't know what they expect us to do – we were instructed to guard the tomb, not break the seal and roll the immovable stone away so some silly women can put spices on a dead body. There is no way we can roll that stone away, anyway. We would have had to get more soldiers to come.

But, we didn't have to. The largest, brightest, most terrifying being I have ever seen does it instead. He drops out of the sky, pushes the stone aside as if it were a pebble, and sits on it. Light comes off of him, streaming in all directions. He is as bright as the sun. He is so bright, I can't look at him. And he is so terrifying, I faint.

Yes, I faint, along with the other soldiers that are with me. I don't know how long we are out, but it is long enough.

I sit up and groan. I nudge the soldier next to me. "Get up!" I say. "We are in trouble."

The tomb is wide open – the stone sitting uselessly off to the side. The tomb is empty. The women are gone. And, thankfully, that huge, shining creature is gone as well.

We look at each other helplessly. "Now what are we to do?" the soldier next to me demands. "We could be executed for this! What happened, anyway? Did you see that shining man?"

He is assaulting my ears with questions. And I can't answer any of them. I am perfectly aware that we could be executed. At the very least, we will be whipped and demoted. How are we to explain this?

"We must go to the chief priests and tell them what happened," I say. My voice sounds calm, but I am not.

"You may do that if you like," my companion says. "Me, I am leaving this place as quickly as I can." He races off in the opposite direction.

I look at the remaining soldiers. Wordlessly, they nod their heads. We begin trudging toward the city.

***

"And that is what happened." I finish my speech before the chief priests and the elders. I have been speaking in a monotone, with my head down. I cannot look at any of them. I am expecting to be seized at any moment and dragged out into the courtyard.

The courtyard…it still bears traces of His blood.

But, no one seizes us. The chief priests have their heads together. They are hastily discussing our fate. We look at each other warily. Perhaps it will not be as bad as we think.

One of the elders hurriedly leaves the room. He comes back with a large sack. He dips his hand into the sack and pulls out gold pieces. He begins distributing the gold among all of us. We are astonished.

The chief priest in charge says, "Take this money. If anyone questions you, tell them his disciples came and stole his body during the night while you were asleep."

I feel anger, disbelief, shame, sorrow, disgust…they are asking us to lie? Not only that, they are bribing us to lie? How can I do this?

"I am a soldier of Rome," I hear myself saying. All eyes turn

89

slowly toward me. I don't care.

"I have been trained from the beginning to be honest and to conduct myself without reproach. This Man was not stolen by His disciples. You know it, and I know it. I told you what happened! I told you the creature of light rolled the stone away -"

I am not allowed to finish. The one in charge gets up and thrusts his finger in my face. "You'll take the money and you will shut your mouth!" he hisses. He whirls around and looks at the other soldiers. "You will all do what you have been told! Does anyone else wish to argue?"

No one does. No one can take his eyes off of the shiny gold coins in his hand.

I leave the room. I walk, then I start running. I run and run until I reach my house.

It is still early in the morning, but my wife is up, busy in the kitchen. She smiles as I burst through the door.

"I was not expecting you so soon, dear one," she says. "Please sit down; I will make you some breakfast."

I sit down. I place the gold coins in a neat stack on the table. Then I put my head down on my arms, and I begin to weep.

Why did they send us to the garden at night? He was in the

temple almost every day, preaching. Why did they send six hundred of us? Why did they crucify Him? What did He do? Why order soldiers to guard a dead man's tomb?

If I had known who He was...if I had realized what was happening...

But I hadn't. I just did my duty. To me, He had been just another military assignment.

My wife is alarmed. "Dearest, what is it?" She comes to my side and strokes my hair. "Do tell me what is wrong."

How can I tell her what is wrong? What do I say to her?

I try to tell her what happened. I stumble over my words. I finally tell her that we are leaving, and going to another city far, far away. I tell her we are leaving tonight, and to gather the things we will need to take with us.

I think she understands. She looks at me with such tenderness in her eyes. "I am proud of you," she tells me.

So, we leave after dark. I turn for one last look. The last thing I see is a stack of gold coins on the table.

We are not taking those with us.

Behind the word: John 18:1 – 6, Matthew 28: 1 – 1

The end